THE BRAGGING BALLOON

Sir Charlie Brown

Pharos Books

ISBN: 978-93-5546-174-2
eISBN: 978-93-5546-175-9

© Publishers

Publisher: Pharos Books (P) Ltd.
Plot No.-55, Main Mother Dairy Road
Pandav Nagar, East Delhi-110092 (India)
Phone: +014049995474
WhatsApp: +014049995474
E-mail: sales@pharosbooks.in
Website: www.pharosbooks.in
Edition: 2022

The Bragging Balloon
Author: Sir Charlie Brown

Dedication

Dedicated to my wife, Cova Jean Brown who encouraged me to make illustrations in the book.

At this point, I would love to dedicate my books to all the employees and sailors from 2003-2017 who encouraged me in getting this book published. Especially, Santa Espinosa and James Alva who loved to watch me draw.

I would like to thank my former place of work, Eagle Foods of Lindenhurst, IL and Sandy Seely and Jackie Sagel. I would also like to thank my publisher, Mahip Bhatia for supporting me and helping me in getting my books published.

Sir Charlie Brown

Out in the east, lay a small town that very few people knew about. In fact, if it wasn't for its small factory that produced plastic balloons, no one, but the locals would know that it ever existed. Coming down the assembly line one could see an assortment of colorful balloons: reds, blues, greens and yellows. All these items manufactured here were considered nothing better than plastic because they were simply lying there. That was until someone would come along who would know how to motivate these deflated items. They would need to place a tube of air and pump them up. In some ways, it looked like gossipers who had filled their heads with hot air.

Interested in listening to the conversation of others, a hand snatched him off the shelf and threw him on the checkout lanes conveyor belt. He was scanned and soon was in the hands of a little girl who opened the package and pulled the yellow balloon out.

It was an opportunity, the balloon had been hoping for a long time. Soon he was filled with helium and was in the hands of a little girl who was holding his future in the string. He wondered when and how would he get free of the strings of this world? He just had to wait patiently.

In the meantime, the girl who was holding her father's hand had entered the park which was situated near her apartment.

The yellow balloon watched the pigeons as they descended to the ground. It seemed to the balloon that they had bowed before him. Actually, they were picking up seeds from the ground that the girl's father threw down for them.

"Well, they sure know royalty when they see it," the balloon thought.

The little girl holding onto the balloon soon got up and walked back to her apartment heading through the path lined up with trees.

"This ungrateful girl has no reason to walk in dangerous zones like this dragging me with her. I have to dodge all these pointy branches just to survive! If I were on my own, I'd show them how to treat royalty."

"I showed them. Those bullies with pointed sticks. They tried to do me in, that proves I have royal plastic in my material." Since the balloon had been dragged several times, so while crossing the street he slowly turned around

to see the trees behind him. As he stuck his tongue out to say that he had victory over those bullies, he noticed the toy store window and all those deflated plastic from where he had come. "I'll never go back to being one of them," he said.

"I'm going to learn a lot so that I never have to return to those bunch of deflates," he said repulsively.

Crossing the street he was hit with an updraft, an upward current of air, which pushed him higher into the air but the little girl held tight to the other end of the string and so the yellow balloon remained floating above the girl's head

He laughed to himself, "even the wind can't push me around. The sad thing is that, I can't prove my worth in this world as long as I'm tied to that string and as long as she holds the other end of this string. She's the one controlling me."

As the father took out his wallet to take out the key card that would unlock the door, it slipped from his fingers and fell to the ground. Immediately the father and the little girl bent over to fetch it which ended up in bumping their heads together. The shock from the bump opened the little girl's hand that held the string and suddenly the yellow balloon was free.

The balloon couldn't believe what had just happened.

He was free! Free of the bond that held him back from doing just what he had wanted to do. Free to do whatever he pleased! Free to head to the top power! Free to talk as much as he wanted to, and no one would tell him to stop.

Yes sir, that balloon was free to brag about anything.
I mean, talk about anything and everything he wanted.

As the balloon rose higher, he suddenly came across a window with a fish looking at the bright round shape floating skyward. Through the water all things took on a different form.

The fish, being a fish, ignored the balloon. This annoyed the round inflated plastic for some reason. "What does a fish know in any case? They have no respect what others have gone through in this world and lead the way like I have."

"It just goes to show that some creatures have no respect for royalty, such as I. If only they knew what I've gone through to get to where I am now. But, I'm still not going to let that stop me. I'm heading for the top and I refuse to let them hold me back."

The balloon floated upward past a window on another floor. Here lay a sleeping cat sunning himself. Slowly it lifted its head and saw the bright yellow balloon. Immediately, he jumped to his feet, arched his back and hissed at the object floating upward.

"What have you got to be afraid of? I fought off trees and air pockets just to be who I am," the balloon bragged.

As the balloon rose higher he mumbled to himself,
"What a dumb animal that was. How can anyone be afraid

of a wonderful thing as I?" The balloon continued to float
up to another window that was on the top floor of the
building.

The last window in the top floor of the building was extremely noisy with barking dogs. The balloon rudely remarked, "How dare they yell at me? Dumb animals, Why? If it weren't for me they would be just a nothing. I'm royalty, I'm headed for bigger and better things, unlike you who bark for no reason."

Rising further in the air and reaching on top of the building the balloon noticed some birds sitting on the edge. He once again began bragging about himself. "Did you know I was created in a royal factory? Then I had to fight off several trees and their pointy branches. I was tossed around by the wind. Escaped a little girl's hold on me. Then I had to fight off this evil looking fish. I had a narrow escape from a scary looking cat. Then I fought off these dogs with teeth. I am now headed to royalty and higher positions."

The yellow balloon continued to brag of things he had never participated in and created stories that were small to tell but made them into a mountain. Finally, a bird flew up to this balloon and began to squawk at his inflated yellow plastic.

Caught off guard by the sudden squawking of the pigeon, he had no other choice but to listen.

"How dare you talk only of yourself. I this, and I that. You act like you're the only thing in the world that has ever done anything. There are others who have done a great amount of things more than you, but you don't see them bragging about themselves. One of these days Mr. Balloon you will find no one listening to you uncontrolled yakking, so you might as well quit while the air inside you is still there."

Saying all this the bird flew away, leaving the balloon speechless.

Do you think the balloon took the friendly advise of the bird? I would say not. He just turned his back on the bird and continued to float upward still talking about himself.

Now, the balloon realized that he was no longer a toy balloon capable to take on the world with his bragging. He realized that he had become the size of a weather balloon on his way to becoming a blimp. All his tall tales gained him nothing.

By the time he realized how wrong his bragging had been it was almost too late. Instead of yakking about himself he could have been encouraging others or build-up confidence in those who were too timid to try, or for that matter, show how fear to try something new is bad, or never be afraid to make mistakes because out of these errors comes success. He and his big mouth ... what a waste of time!

POP

www.ingramcontent.com/pod-product-compliance
Lightning Source LLC
LaVergne TN
LVHW080516200726
843507LV00008B/1117